To all who blazed a trail for me to have this chance to bring
holiday magic through ballet –C.N.

To Charlotte Nebres and all artists who give old stories
new life and get new stories started –S.W.

For Suzanna –A.M.

Text copyright © 2021 by Charlotte Nebres
Jacket art and interior illustrations copyright © 2021 by Alea Marley
Illustrations on pages 36–37 copyright © 2021 by Charlotte Nebres

All rights reserved. Published in the United States by Random House Children's Books,
a division of Penguin Random House LLC, New York.

Random House and the colophon are registered trademarks of Penguin Random House LLC.

Visit us on the Web! rhcbooks.com

Educators and librarians, for a variety of teaching tools, visit us at RHTeachersLibrarians.com

Library of Congress Cataloging-in-Publication Data
Names: Nebres, Charlotte, author. | Marley, Alea, illustrator.
Title: Charlotte and the nutcracker : the true story of a girl who made ballet history / Charlotte Nebres ;
with Sarah Warren ; illustrated by Alea Marley.
Description: First edition. | New York : Random House, 2021. | Summary: "A picture book that
weaves together Charlotte Nebres's life story as a young ballerina with the
classic holiday tale of the Nutcracker." —Provided by publisher.
Identifiers: LCCN 2020046477 (print) | LCCN 2020046478 (ebook) |
ISBN 978-0-593-37490-0 (hardcover) | ISBN 978-0-593-37491-7 (library binding) |
ISBN 978-0-593-37492-4 (epub)
Subjects: LCSH: Nebres, Charlotte—Juvenile fiction. | CYAC: Nebres, Charlotte—Fiction. |
Ballet—Fiction. | Nutcracker (Choreographic work)—Fiction. | Christmas—Fiction.
Classification: LCC PZ7.1.N383 Ch 2021 (print) | LCC PZ7.1.N383 (ebook) | DDC [E]—dc23

The artist used Procreate to create the illustrations for this book.
The text of this book is set in 18-point Isabel Condensed Light.

MANUFACTURED IN CHINA
10 9 8 7 6 5 4 3 2 1
First Edition

CHARLOTTE AND THE Nutcracker

The True Story of a Girl Who Made Ballet History

Charlotte Nebres

with Sarah Warren

Illustrations by
Alea Marley

Random House ⌂ New York

It isn't quite Christmas–not yet. But Charlotte gets the best gift she can imagine: her first ballet class.
Music.
Dancing.
Dreaming.
Charlotte and her sister laugh, spin, and hop!

Eventually, Charlotte grows strong enough to balance beside the barre. She stands tall, just like her teachers.

They make Charlotte feel at home: "Hello, Shiny!" they say.
She stands even taller.

After class, going to the ballet is a treat!
On special days, the theater looks like church
and the audience feels like family.

Today is one of those days.

Charlotte perches on her velvety chair.
There's the ballerina everyone's talking about!
Her brown skin glows bright in the stage
lamps. This ballerina looks like family.
Charlotte can see herself–she can see herself
getting up on that stage, too.

Dancing on a big stage–like her favorite ballerina–takes practice. Each day after school, Charlotte races to ballet.

Charlotte stretches like a butterfly.
Then she gets started:
Rond de jambe.
Soutenu.
Adagio.

Charlotte stacks new movements
together like blocks. She adjusts her
long arms.
Not quite. Almost. There!

Some dancers from Charlotte's school get to perform with the New York City Ballet.
Charlotte hopes to be picked someday, so she always does her best.

Day by day ... Charlotte's best gets a little better. Day by day ...
that's how she'll be ready for someday.

Charlotte learned about hard work from her family, who made it possible for new dreams to come true. A part in *The Nutcracker* is Charlotte's dream—getting to celebrate Christmas for months!

Finally, Charlotte is called to audition. She adjusts her arms.

Not quite. Almost. There!

Charlotte can't believe it when she gets the news. "I'm Marie," she
whispers. *The hero of the story!*

They say it's the first time the New York City Ballet will have a Black
girl playing Marie. *Huh,* she thinks, *that seems a little late.*

Now Charlotte will be the one onstage at Lincoln Center. She knows how good it feels to see someone who looks like you up there. Maybe other boys and girls will feel the way she did:

Welcomed.
Beautiful.
Ready to dance!

Playing Marie takes practice. Charlotte is bringing a fantasy to life.

When the curtain goes up during rehearsal,
she counts *1...2...3...4...5...6...7...8.*
She pretends to yawn. She stretches. She opens her
eyes.

On opening night, what will she see?

The night of the first show, older dancers play cards and draw red cheeks on toy soldiers while Charlotte paints her antsy energy away.

"Places!" announces the stage manager. It's time.

Violins play. The curtain goes up.
Charlotte's heart pounds. She feels her skin glow bright in the light.
Now *she's* the ballerina everyone's talking about.

Thousands of people wait to see what she'll do next. She can only pick out a few faces, but she finds the one she's looking for: Mama. Charlotte winks.

Charlotte travels straight into
the wide-open joy of Christmas.
Toe, ball, heel.
Toe, ball, heel.
Toe, ball, heel.

Mice creep across the stage.
The Nutcracker lifts his sword.
Charge!

She and her
prince wave goodbye.
Bravo!

Snowflakes flutter, float, and fly
as she claims a frosting-covered
throne.

For weeks, *The Nutcracker* puts audiences in the holiday spirit. Then Charlotte celebrates Christmas Eve with the people she loves most.

At home, she breathes in the toasted, sugar-soaked, fruity comfort of Mom's baking.

Her grandfather's stew simmers so long, she could spoon a spicy bite right out of the air.

Charlotte and her grandmother use banana leaves to wrap bundles of dough filled with spicy meat.

Together, the family makes a holiday feast.

Charlotte's house becomes a dazzling island in
their sleeping neighborhood.
Dancing.
Strumming.
Drumming.

The next morning, they greet the holiday with music. *Hello, Christmas!*
Charlotte races to the presents. A snow globe!

Charlotte and her brother and sister
search the prickly branches of their
twinkling tree. *Aha!* The hidden pickle.

After dinner, Charlotte's dad surprises them with a velvet pouch. Inside is a peppermint-candy pig!

They take turns with a small silver hammer. *Tap . . . tap . . . tap . . . SMASH!* Winning the biggest piece? That's Christmas!

Charlotte wonders, *What does the holiday mean to Marie?*
Music.
Dancing.
Dreaming.

Marie is someone who experiences magic. Charlotte understands—because of *The Nutcracker*, she gets to experience magic over and over again.

When I was eleven years old, I was cast as Marie in George Balanchine's *The Nutcracker*. I've always loved this holiday classic and the story of Marie: a little girl who drifts into a magical dreamland on Christmas Eve. Being Marie was a dream come true for me! It felt like Christmas every day, and I still carry that magic with me now.

It was surprising to learn that I was the first Black ballerina to perform this role with the New York City Ballet. I'm honored to be a part of bringing diverse representation to this art form. I hope my casting will create more opportunities for diverse dancers and audiences to be welcomed and celebrated in the ballet world!

Holiday traditions like going to see *The Nutcracker* are very special to my family. Like many families, we have holiday traditions that reflect a dynamic blend of people with a diverse heritage. My family has roots in the islands of Trinidad and the Philippines. We keep that heritage alive during the holidays by sharing the food and culture. What traditions make your holiday celebrations special? Do you incorporate your heritage in your traditions? However you celebrate, I am wishing you a very happy holiday!

xoxo,
Charlotte